# Cupcake

## A Journey to Special

### Charise Mericle Harper

Disney • Hyperion Books
New York

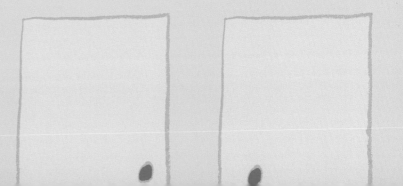

For Henry, who loves all cupcakes,
and, because he likes to share,
Owen will help eat them up too!

Text and illustrations © 2010 by Charise Mericle Harper

For information address Disney • Hyperion Books, 114 Fifth Avenue, New York, New York 10011-5690.
First Edition
10 9 8 7 6 5 4 3 2
H106-9333-5-12350
Printed in Malaysia
Reinforced binding
ISBN 978-1-4231-1897-8
Library of Congress Cataloging-in-Publication Data on file.
Visit www.hyperionbooksforchildren.com

Book design by Teresa Kietlinski Dikun
Text set in Coffeedance and Journal
Art was drawn by hand and colored in Photoshop.

One day, in a big bowl, flour, sugar, eggs, milk,
and baking powder were all mixed together.

And then, with just the right amount of baking in a toasty hot oven . . .

. . . Cupcake was born.

After a special coat of icing, Vanilla Cupcake was creamy white, perfectly plain, and most certainly delicious.

Being a friendly sort of cupcake, he quickly introduced himself to all his new brothers and sisters.

There was . . .

Happy-Face Cupcake

A smile a day makes the blues go away.

Pink Princess Cupcake

Charmed, I'm sure.

Chocolaty Chocolate Cupcake

It's chocorific to meet you.

Cupcake felt special to be part of such a large
and colorful family.

Nobody picked me.
I'm too creamy white and plain!

But by the end of the day, Cupcake wasn't feeling very special anymore. He was sitting on the plate all alone.

A candle that was close by heard Cupcake crying and hopped over.

What's wrong?

"I know how you feel," said Candle, and then he told Cupcake all about *his* fancy brothers and sisters.

Let's see, there's . . .

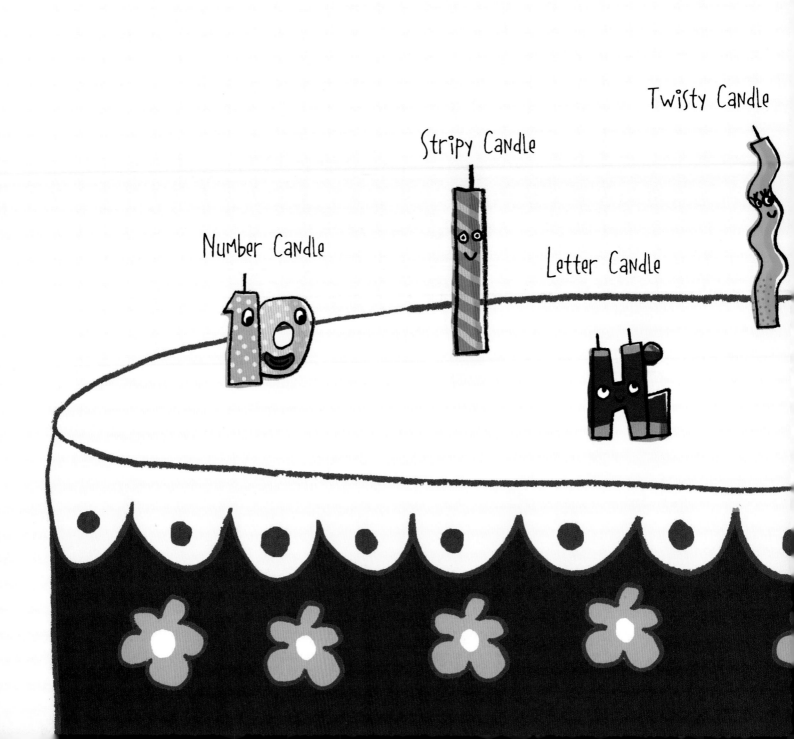

Number Candle

Stripy Candle

Letter Candle

Twisty Candle

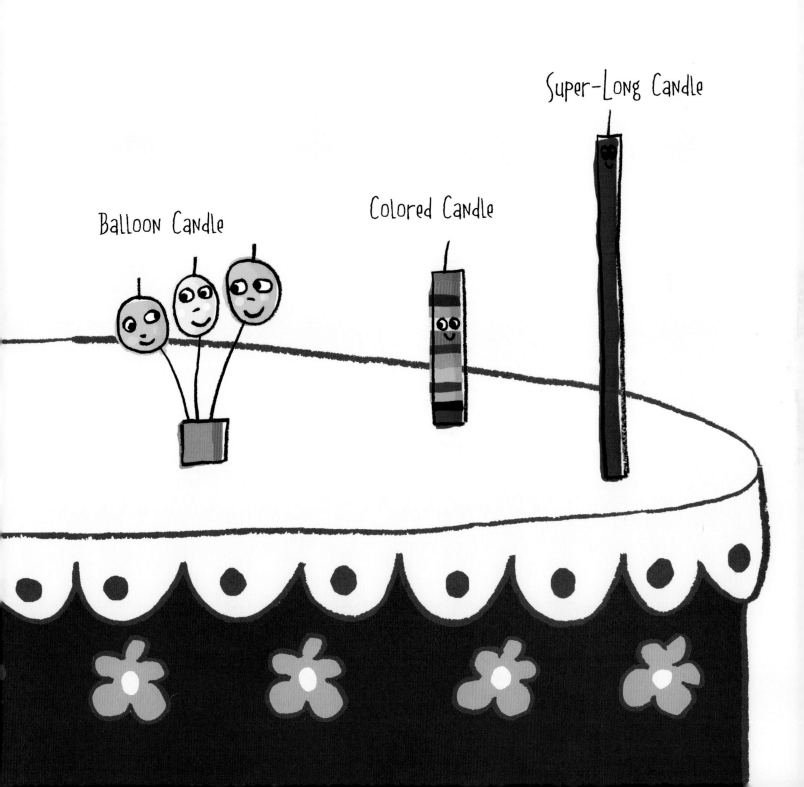

Balloon Candle

Colored Candle

Super-Long Candle

Now *both* Cupcake and Candle were feeling sad.

That is, until Candle had a **big idea.**

Hey, you JUST need a special topping.

"You're RIGHT!" said Cupcake. Candle hopped off to find the something special.

WOW!
He is so bright.

Candle had all sorts of suggestions.

Pickles!

"TOO salty!" said Cupcake.

Pancakes,

an egg,

PEAS.

And then . . .

A Squirrel!

Ughh! Too furry!

"I'm sorry," said Candle.
"I really thought we'd find something special."

"Look!" said Candle. "What's that?"

Where? Where?

UP there ON YOUR head.

"There's something in here," said Candle.

"Wait! I've got it!" said Candle.

# Recipe for Deliciously Plain VANILLA CUPCAKES

## INGREDIENTS:

2 cups all-purpose flour

3 teaspoons baking powder

½ teaspoon salt

½ cup butter

1 ½ cups sugar

4 eggs, separated

1 cup 2% milk

1 ½ teaspoons vanilla

## PREPARATION:

1 • Preheat oven until toasty (350°).

2 • Line cupcake pans with paper liners.

3 • Combine flour, baking powder, and salt, set aside.

4 • In new bowl combine butter, 1 cup of sugar, egg yolks, milk, vanilla, and a little bit of love.

5 • Now add dry ingredients to this mix.

6 • Mix at low speed for 2 minutes. Scrape bowl.

7 • Whip up remaining sugar with the egg whites, mixing at high speed until fluffy and smooth.

8 • Fold this into batter. It is going to be yummy!

9 • Fill liners one half to two thirds full of batter. Do not overfill.

10 • Bake 20 to 25 minutes or until toothpick inserted in centers comes out clean.

11 • Cool 10 minutes in pans, then remove and place on a wire rack to cool completely.

12 • Frost with Deliciously Plain Buttercream Frosting and ENJOY!

# Deliciously Plain BUTTERCREAM FROSTING

## INGREDIENTS:

½ cup butter, softened

4 cups powdered or confectioners' sugar

¼ teaspoon salt

4–5 tablespoons milk

2 teaspoons vanilla

## PREPARATION:

1 • In large bowl, cream butter until very fluffy.

2 • Add part of the sugar and the salt and beat again.

3 • Continue adding sugar and milk in small batches, alternately, beating until very fluffy.

4 • Stir in vanilla.

5 • Frost your Deliciously Plain Cupcakes and eat! YUM.